BIG ★ KID POWER

Bye-Bye BINKY

Maria van Lieshout

chronicle books · san francisco

When I was a baby, I cried a lot.

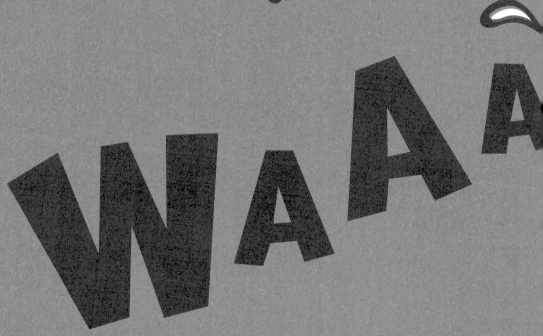

WaAA

I cried when
I was tired . . .

BOOHOO HOOo

and when
I was hungry.

NEEEEEH

And I cried when I was upset,

WEEEEEEEEEEEH

UNLESS...

. . . I had my binky.

I LOVED MY BINKY.

Do I still have a binky?

NO,
BIG KIDS
DON'T NEED
A BINKY.

Big kids ask for

HUGS.

When I am tired, I cuddle with my lovey.

When I am sad,
I snuggle with
a friend.

When I am hungry,
I ask for a snack.

But what should
I do with my binky?

I'll give it to a little baby.
When the baby cries,

WAAAAAAH

he can use my binky.

Bye-bye binky!

Bye-bye
little baby!

I'M A BIG KID!

As a baby, my son Max loved his binky. And so did I. It soothed him back to sleep after he woke us in the middle of the night (for the fifth time!).

But the time comes to let binky go. And when that time came for us, I decided to find out how other parents had handled this milestone. I was inspired by the many ways parents encourage their kids to bid binky farewell. And I noticed that the one thing many of them had in common was a ritual of some sort. The ritual celebrates that children have achieved something important. They are now a BIG KID and can conquer any challenge that comes their way.

That's what BIG KID POWER is all about.